How "I" Died

Mansi Rajan

About the Author

Mansi Rajan is a new budding writer born in India on **24 September 1999** she made her debut in 2019 she wrote her first book at the age of 20 and got it published at her 21 she wrote about her experiences with social problems to defend the legitimacy of pain she says that our pain doesn't come because of our lifestyle and it is also not taken away by our lifestyle some emotionally arresting memoir reveal her experiences about life. before this she has also written two books Truth is that new authors are always exciting to read. And the caveat is – as long as they bring something new to the world of fiction, non-fiction or socially.

I

"I Stands for Ego"

The ego plays a crucial role in defining who we think we are and how it shapes our perception of the world. Sometimes we forget difference between ego and self respect I.e. When you avoid someone without any second thoughts when they point at your *mistakes*, that is your ego. When you avoid someone after thinking for a while when they question your *character*, that is your self respect.

Ego is about establishing your importance or superiority, usually in one sense or the another you are comparing yourself to another and wanted to prove yourself to be better. Self respect is about maintaining your confidence and boundaries in situations when someone is treating you unfairly.

We should understand that if we lose our ego, we would get more opportunities, but if we lose our Self-respect, we lose everything. You will stop respecting yourself and instead start hating yourself resulting in depression. When I overhear someone abusing me or making fun of me, I do get hurt for a moment, then I start thinking about all the positive things of my life and about myself, like... I self praise in my mind and become normal in few minutes. I feel that there is no point to take it to my ego. According to me, my self-respect is in my hands. Only I can tamper my self-respect. If someone else are trying to hurt it, then they are only hurting my ego. When I myself don't worry about my ego getting hurt, then there is no point that they can hurt my self respect.

I wasn't always like this though. I learnt this trick after getting hurt for many years. I realised that I was wasting my emotions in a negative way which otherwise I could have invested in somewhere else, doing something more productive and positive."**When you go to unnecessary places you will get to hear unwanted words"**

That is, in a negative environment, you cannot expect a positive vibe. So, to put in simpler words;

Ego is when you don't want to listen to someone pointing out your mistakes and correct yourself, don't want to learn from your mistakes and grow as a person both personally and professionally.

Self-respect is when you listen to someone pointing out your mistakes, analyse it and if you find that they are right, then correct yourself and try not to repeat those mistakes again and grow as a person both personally and professionally.

Ego is when you only think of winning by running irrespective of the road or the path and not worrying if it is correct or not.

Self-respect is when you think of winning in the correct way, by running on the correct road and path.

Let me explain this by a story :-

A young man asked a monk, 'What is ego?'

The monk in turn asked him, 'Who are you?'

'Well,' replied the young man, giving his name, 'Mohan.'

'I am not asking your name; I want to know who are you?' countered the monk.

'I am a student', said the young man.

'But that is your present station or "profession" in life; my question is—who are you?'

The young man thought for a while and then said, 'I am the son of so-and-so.'

'That is your relation with your parents,' smiled the monk.

'I am a Bengali', said the young man.

'That is your mother-tongue'

'I am a Hindu and an Indian.'

'That is your religion and your nationality.'

'I am a human being,' the young man reached his wit's end.

'Now, you are referring to the species— the Homo sapiens. Who are you?'

The young man had nothing more to say. 'Well, that is what Vedanta teaches,' continued the monk,

The Vedanta says that man's deepest core or substance within, is unconditioned by any description and that unconditioned substance is called Atma or Self. The Atma is what a man is. Ego is what he appears to be. Atma is true, ego is false. Atma is never born nor dies; ego comes into being through ignorance and dies when knowledge dawns in a person.
Ego is basically identity. Anything that is rigid has a side effect of restricting the flow of life, resisting it, on some level. There are many layers of ego, and it's delusional to think one's ego is completely destroyed in self-realization.

In the separated state, we identify with our **mental self-image.** Some people think the separated state is the state of identification with the body, but it's not true. Such descriptions come from a realized state, yes, but not from complete realization (see below). If that was true, people would never say "I have a body", they would only say "I am the body". But for most people, "I have a body" is a much more natural thing to say. So this "I", which "has" a body, this idea of yourself doesn't actually exist anywhere but in your mind, and it's your mental identity, your self-image. This identity corresponds to the "bull" in the famous Ten Bulls pictures of Zen. There are all kinds of clinging to what type of person you are or should be, how life should be for you, how others should treat you, what is "good" and "bad", "right" and "wrong" etc. **This is the separated state.** Most people are in this state and they recognize and relate to each other's egos.

In self-realization, this identity is seen to be false. One's identity then moves to **Consciousness**, Love, Being, God. One basically becomes love itself as the ultimate witness of Existence. Everything is beautiful, there's joy everywhere, and tons of compassion to other sentient beings that haven't yet realized the simple truth of life that everything is love. This is sometimes called God Consciousness, and it's the state of a Bodhisattva, or Jesus Christ. It's also referred to as "loving awareness", or Reality/Consciousness/Bliss, Sat-Chit-Ananda. This is Atman, the soul. Osho's "the death of the ego is the birth of the soul" refers to this state. In the Ten Bulls, it corresponds to, "The Bull Transcended". Sayings like "I am not my body", "you are me" come from this place. There is no doer, Being moves you. There's still clinging to Being, to life, to love and beauty at this state. **This is "I am", the beginning of non-duality.** It is possible to recognize someone in this state since he embodies unconditional love.

But underneath all that love and beauty there's still pain, hatred and the fear of non-existence. So, in what is most often called enlightenment, even this identity is seen to be false, and so the identity moves to **Brahman,** the totality of all existence. Atman and Brahman are seen to be one. This identity is way beyond the manifested consciousness, it is unmanifest. This is the state of non-Being, Buddhahood, complete aloneness. Sayings like "I am nothing" come from this place. Maharishi's "where can I go, I am always here" also comes from this place. There is no love, no beauty here, just emptiness, Shunyata, because only ugliness can remember beauty and only hatred can remember love. As nothingness, one becomes infinite. All emotion is transcended here. One is completely at peace with his fate to dissolve into nothingness from which one has appeared. This is sometimes called the Cosmic Consciousness, the ultimate level of consciousness. In the Ten Bulls, it corresponds to #8, "Both Bull and Self Transcended", an empty circle. There is no doer, things just happen. It is sometimes called The Absolute, but it's not The Absolute. There is still a subtle clinging to non-

Being, to infinity, and to death at this state. **This is "I'm not", the deepest state of non-duality.** It becomes very hard to recognize someone at this state because only a subtle hint of ego remains here and it's very hard to relate to such person.

But that's also not all, because the identity of Brahman is also a false identity. Once it is seen, Being and non-Being, manifest and unmanifest are seen to be one. There is no more clinging to life as one truly accepted death, and there is no more clinging to death as a subtle hope that some experience of Brahmanic bliss lies beyond it. **This is The Absolute.** In the Ten Bulls, it corresponds to #9, "Reaching the Source". Osho called it "beyond enlightenment" and described it as "my body and my Spirit are finally one". In Hinduism, they sometimes refer to it as Para Brahman. Euphoria of existence and emptiness of non-existence merge together. Nothing can be said about this state, because this is when one becomes completely, utterly ordinary again. There's only life, exactly as it is, in its absolute such-ness without either overwhelming love and beauty nor personal detachment of a witness. The identity finally moves to where it belongs - **to the body.** One is simply his body as all other animals are. The human condition is transcended. This is the end of non-duality and infinity, one becomes finite again. Nothing that doesn't exist in the physical world, including Brahman, exists anymore. One becomes the doer again, just rid of all the illusions of life. This is what the last picture in the Ten Bulls, "Return to Society" is about. **This is Enlightenment.** It is strictly impossible to recognize someone at this state, because his identity is his body and everyone has a body. Even people at various stages of non-duality can't relate to such a person, and he appears completely ignorant to them.

In the words of Kabir, *"self-realization is when the dew drops into the ocean and you can't find it anymore; in enlightenment the ocean drops back into the dewdrop and you can't find the ocean anymore"*.

Of course, not everyone's unfolding of the dream will be linear as I described it here, and mine wasn't either. It can be a messy process, but all of that will become obvious in due time if you go through it till the end. The lesson, as usual, is not to cling to anything newly found and always be willing to go deeper and deeper into the truth of your nature, the state of the ultimate relaxation, the ultimate let go.

II

<u>I am beacause of me</u>

The phrase "I am because of me" carries deep personal meaning, as it suggests a self-driven, independent journey of identity and growth.

"I Am Because of Me: The Power of Self-Determination in Shaping Who We Become"

- The role of self-awareness in personal transformation.

Self-reflection: Unlocking the Path to Personal Growth and Self-Awareness In our fast-paced and ever-evolving world, the journey of self-discovery and personal growth has become increasingly vital. At the heart of this transformative process lies the powerful practice of self-reflection. It is through introspection and thoughtful contemplation that we can gain a deeper understanding of ourselves, uncover our true potential, and foster meaningful change in our lives. In this article, we will explore the significance of self-reflection in personal transformation and self-awareness, acknowledging its pivotal role in shaping our paths to growth and fulfillment.

A. Definition of Self-Reflection

Before delving into its significance, let us first grasp the essence of self-reflection. Simply put, self-reflection is the deliberate act of examining one's thoughts, emotions, and actions with a keen and unbiased eye. It involves stepping back from the whirlwind of daily life and creating a space for introspection — an opportunity to connect with our inner selves and gain valuable insights into our own experiences.

B. Importance of Personal Transformation and Self-Awareness

Personal transformation, the process of evolving and becoming the best version of ourselves, holds immense significance in our lives. It enables us to break free from self-imposed limitations, embrace new perspectives, and explore uncharted territories. Similarly, self-awareness acts as a guiding compass, allowing us to navigate through life with clarity and authenticity. By understanding our strengths, weaknesses, values, and aspirations, we can make conscious choices that align with our true selves and lead to genuine fulfillment.

C. Thesis Statement: Self-Reflection's Crucial Role

D. Within this context, self-reflection emerges as an invaluable tool, serving as the bridge that connects personal transformation and self-awareness. By engaging in self-reflection, we embark on a journey of self-discovery that unravels the layers of our being, enabling us to grow, adapt, and thrive. It is through this introspective process that we gain the wisdom and insights necessary to make conscious changes, develop a deep sense of self-awareness, and ultimately transform our lives. As we delve further into this exploration, we will uncover the components of self-reflection, examine its transformative power, explore techniques for effective introspection, and address the challenges one might encounter on this profound journey of self-discovery. By the end of this article, we hope to inspire you to embrace self-reflection as a lifelong practice, empowering you to embark on a transformative path toward personal growth and self-awareness.

II. Understanding Self-Reflection

A. Definition and Components of Self-Reflection

Self-reflection, at its core, is the conscious process of turning our attention inward and examining our thoughts, emotions, and actions. It involves a deliberate and honest assessment of our experiences, beliefs, values, and goals. Within the realm of self-reflection, several components shape the depth and effectiveness of the practice. These components include self-awareness, self-observation, self-evaluation, and self-questioning. Self-awareness is the foundation of self-reflection, as it involves being attuned to our own inner state and recognizing the thoughts, feelings, and patterns that influence our behavior. Self-observation entails keenly observing ourselves in different situations, noticing our reactions, and gaining insights into our behavioral patterns. Self-evaluation involves objectively assessing our actions, choices, and outcomes to understand their impact on our lives. Lastly, self-questioning involves posing thoughtful inquiries to ourselves, aiming to deepen our understanding and challenge our assumptions.

B. Benefits of Engaging in Self-Reflection

Engaging in self-reflection offers a multitude of benefits that can positively impact our personal growth and well-being. Firstly, self-reflection cultivates self-awareness, allowing us to gain a deeper understanding of our values, strengths, weaknesses, and motivations. By recognizing our patterns of behavior and thought, we can make conscious choices aligned with our authentic selves. Furthermore, self-reflection enhances emotional intelligence, enabling us to better understand and manage our emotions. Through introspection, we can identify triggers, explore the root causes of our emotional responses, and develop healthier coping mechanisms. In addition, self-reflection fosters personal growth by providing opportunities for learning and self-improvement. By examining our past experiences, both successes, and failures, we can extract valuable lessons and apply them to future endeavors. This iterative process of self-assessment and growth propels us forward on our journey of personal development.

C. The link between Self-Reflection and Personal Growth

Self-reflection and personal growth are intrinsically interconnected. By engaging in self-reflection, we actively participate in our own personal growth journey. Through introspection, we gain insights into our strengths and weaknesses, which enables us to focus on areas for improvement and development. Self-reflection also helps us identify and challenge limiting beliefs and thought patterns that may hinder our progress. Moreover, self-reflection encourages goal-setting and aligning our actions with our values. By taking the time to reflect on our aspirations and values, we can ensure that our choices and behaviors are in harmony with our authentic selves. This alignment fuels personal growth and facilitates a sense of fulfillment and purpose in our lives. In essence, self-reflection serves as a catalyst for personal growth by providing the self-awareness, learning opportunities, and mindset shifts necessary to evolve and transform. It empowers us to make conscious choices, embrace change, and continuously strive towards becoming the best version of ourselves. By embracing self-reflection, we embark on a profound journey of self-discovery and personal growth, setting the stage for the transformative power that lies ahead.

III. Self-Reflection as a Catalyst for Personal Transformation

A. Recognizing strengths and weaknesses

Self-reflection provides a platform for acknowledging and understanding our strengths and weaknesses. Through introspection, we can identify the areas in which we excel, allowing us to leverage those strengths to our advantage. Simultaneously, self-reflection allows us to recognize our limitations and areas that require improvement. This self-awareness empowers us to make informed decisions, seek growth opportunities, and maximize our potential.

B. Identifying limiting beliefs and thought patterns

Self-reflection helps us uncover and challenge the limiting beliefs and thought patterns that may hinder our personal growth. By examining our inner dialogue and belief systems, we can identify negative self-talk, self-doubt, and self-imposed limitations. Through self-reflection, we can replace these limiting beliefs with empowering ones, fostering a mindset conducive to growth and transformation.

C. Setting goals and aligning actions with values

Engaging in self-reflection allows us to clarify our values and aspirations, providing a foundation for setting meaningful goals. By exploring our core values and aligning them with our goals, we can ensure that our actions and decisions are in harmony with our authentic selves. Self-reflection serves as a compass, guiding us to make choices that align with our values and propel us toward personal transformation.

D. Embracing change and seeking personal growth opportunities

Self-reflection encourages us to embrace change and actively seek personal growth opportunities.By examining our experiences, behaviors, and outcomes, we gain insights into areas where change is necessary.

Through self-reflection, we become open to new perspectives, ideas, and experiences that contribute to our personal growth. It fosters a mindset of continuous learning and self-improvement, propelling us toward transformative change. Self-reflection acts as a catalyst for personal transformation by facilitating self-awareness, uncovering limiting beliefs, aligning actions with values, and embracing change. It empowers us to recognize and leverage our strengths, address our weaknesses, and set goals that align with our true selves. By embracing self-reflection, we embark on a transformative journey of personal growth and development.

IV. Self-Reflection and Enhanced Self-Awareness

A. Developing an accurate self-perception Self-reflection plays a crucial role in developing an accurate and authentic self-perception. By taking the time to introspect, we can gain insights into our values, beliefs, strengths, and weaknesses. Through self-reflection, we can align our self-perception with our true selves, free from external influences or societal expectations. This deepened self-awareness allows us to navigate life with authenticity and make choices that align with our genuine identity.

B. Exploring emotions and motivations

Self-reflection invites us to explore our emotions and motivations, delving beneath the surface to understand the driving forces behind our actions. By examining our emotional responses to various situations, we can uncover underlying triggers and gain a deeper understanding of our emotional landscape. This heightened self-awareness allows us to respond to situations more effectively and cultivate emotional intelligence. Through self-reflection, we gain insights into our motivations, desires, and fears, enabling us to make conscious choices that align with our values and aspirations.

C. Recognizing patterns of behavior and their impact

Engaging in self-reflection enables us to recognize patterns of behavior that may have gone unnoticed in our daily lives. By observing our actions and their consequences, we gain a clearer understanding of how our behaviors impact ourselves and those around us. Through self-reflection, we become aware of any detrimental patterns, such as self-sabotage or unhealthy coping mechanisms. This recognition empowers us to make intentional changes, break free from negative cycles, and cultivate healthier and more productive behaviors.

D. Cultivating empathy and understanding toward others

Self-reflection not only enhances our self-awareness but also fosters empathy and understanding toward others. By examining our own thoughts, feelings, and behaviors, we develop a deeper sense of empathy for the experiences of those around us. Through self-reflection, we gain insights into our own biases, judgments, and preconceptions, allowing us to approach others with greater openness and acceptance. This expanded perspective nurtures stronger relationships, fosters effective communication, and promotes a sense of interconnectedness with the world around us.

Self-reflection serves as a powerful tool for enhancing self-awareness by developing an accurate self-perception, exploring emotions and motivations, recognizing behavior patterns, and cultivating empathy towards others. It enables us to better understand ourselves and navigate our interactions with authenticity and empathy, ultimately contributing to personal growth and harmonious relationships.

Techniques for Effective Self-Reflection

A. Journaling and Expressive Writing Journaling and expressive writing are powerful techniques for self-reflection. By putting pen to paper, we create a safe space to express our thoughts, emotions, and experiences without judgment. Through journaling, we can explore our inner world, gain clarity, and discover patterns or insights that may not have been apparent before. Writing allows us to delve deep into our thoughts and reflect on our experiences, providing a tangible record of our growth and transformation.

B. Mindfulness and Meditation Practices

Mindfulness and meditation practices offer a way to cultivate present-moment awareness and foster self-reflection. By dedicating time to quieting the mind and focusing on the present, we can observe our thoughts, emotions, and bodily sensations with curiosity and non-judgment. Mindfulness and meditation provide a mental space for self-reflection, allowing us to gain insights into our inner landscape, notice any habitual thought patterns, and cultivate a greater sense of self-awareness.

C. Seeking Feedback from Trusted Individuals

Seeking feedback from trusted individuals can provide valuable perspectives and insights for self-reflection.Trusted friends, mentors, or family members can offer different viewpoints and observations about our behaviors, strengths, and areas for improvement.Their feedback can serve as a mirror, helping us gain a more comprehensive understanding of ourselves. It is important to choose individuals who provide constructive feedback and have our best interests at heart, fostering a supportive environment for growth and self-reflection.

D. Engaging in Introspective Questioning

E. Introspective questioning involves deliberately asking ourselves thought-provoking questions to stimulate self-reflection. By posing open-ended inquiries, we encourage deep introspection and exploration of our thoughts, beliefs, and motivations. Questions like "What do I truly value in life?" or "What fears are holding me back?" prompt us to examine our inner landscape, challenge assumptions, and gain insights that can drive personal growth. Engaging in introspective questioning opens doors to self-discovery and fosters a greater understanding of ourselves. Effective self-reflection techniques, such as journaling, mindfulness practices, seeking feedback, and introspective questioning, provide intentional spaces for introspection and self-discovery. By incorporating these techniques into our routine, we create opportunities to deepen our self-awareness, gain valuable insights, and navigate our journey of personal transformation with intention and purpose.

F.

III

<u>The Journey Is The Destination</u>

What if the journey is actually more meaningful than the destination?

The journey is what it is, a *journey*. The destination is the *end point* of the journey. If the journey never ends, then you will never reach a destination *until you die.* Where you die will be your *final destination* on this plane of life. A journey is not a destination. There may be many destinations *during* your journey, but *the journey is not a destination.*

Confusing ?? okk let's study this in a simple language .All the labour of man is for his mouth, and yet the appetite is not filled.

Do you perceive what this is telling us? It means ultimately all we are ever doing is laboring for survival. We labor being busy with everything we will ever do in order to fill the mouth. But that's like chasing the tail around without a destination knowing the appetite will return to begin the process over and over and over again. Where is man's final destination but the grave as everyone is heading toward this same hidden place beneath the ground. Then shall the dust return to the earth as it was: and the spirit shall return unto God who gave it. There's no such resting point as one should hope to arrive at some illusionary destination for all to come is vanity and there's nothing waiting for us. We are never the better for all we will ever do. In this way just enjoy the ride as a priveldge in journeying to the grave as the only destination. To satisfy more directly speaking the journey we make is not toward a destination which can be finalized, for as one hurdle is crossed there will more and always be more to cross over.

In track competition the destination is for one to cross the finish line, to either win or not to win. It's running toward the ending line which is the thrill of the journey as its destination. It's man's destiny to journey to the end of life as death is the only destination we will meet and share alike while journeying.

.Imagine that I wanted to write a great novel. Publishing the novel is the 'destination', the end of the journey. The journey would be the process of thinking about the novel, planning it, writing an outline, writing the draft, editing, revising, and all the rest.

Now I've finished. Maybe I didn't actually write a great novel. Maybe it's average, or not very good. However, by going through the process, by taking that journey, I learned a significant amount about myself, my talents, my skills, my patience, and about my ability to accomplish things. The journey was more important than the destination.

Life is living everyday, moment by moment. That is why God's name is, "I AM!" He is the present tense God. This moment, right now! That is all we have!

But, I do believe we must have a hope for a future to keep us going when the moment seems desperate. We wait on God, as we have cried out to Him, for relief. We hope that He will come through and give us His peace! We have seen Him do it in the past, and we pray He has mercy on us now!

Also, it is good to have goals for some future events to keep us having purpose and meaning in life. Otherwise, we might grow lethargic and listless saying, " What does it matter anyways?" Christ gives us a command and a commission to keep us busy while we are journeying here. That is to "Love one another," and to:

> **"Go and make disciples of all nations, baptizing them in the name of the**

Father and of the Son and of the Holy Spirit,

"and teaching them to obey everything I have commanded you."—Matthew 28:19-20

We occupy on this Earth until He comes or we go to meet Him. That is our true destination! We are just sojourning here and pray we can reach as many people as possible with the love and forgiveness of Father God! This place is not our true home. It is with our LORD and Savior Jesus Christ!
But life is not a race to the finish line.

"It's not the destination, it's the journey" is a quote famously attributed to Ralph Waldo Emerson the American philosopher.

Enjoying the journey, 'the getting there', is every bit as important to me as arriving at the destination. There is joy and learning to be taken from every possible moment we live our lives, whether that is inside or outside of work.

You may wonder why I am sharing this today of all days? After all you have already heard quite a lot from me today already! In the work context, I have been very focused on our strategy and whenever we have our town halls and video updates I take the opportunity to not only share the progress we are making but always anchor it back to where we are going and why we are going there (our strategy).

Today you heard from me that we have acquired the Knoldus business, which is a fantastic addition to the Nash Squared family and to NashTech in particular. You will hear more about this as the weeks ahead unfold so I won't write more on that here other than to say that this carries us very much further on the road to delivering our strategy, which is exciting.

Instead I would like to write a little bit on the journey that brought us here. Of course there is a lot of work involved in finding, getting to know and acquiring a business, and it can only ever happen if there is a joint purpose and belief that we are better together and can achieve so much more when combined. It also takes time to get to know each other as people, really understand what our values are, understand how our ways of working and culture could work. Above everything it takes trust.

Hard work aside, the journey to where we have got today has been incredible. After all, some time ago we had never spoken, met or known very much about each other. I often marvel how 8 billion people go about their lives on our planet, all with our own hopes and dreams until one day we meet and only then do we marvel at how this could be, how could we have never known of each other. there are endless differences if we start to write between journey and destination, not about those positions themselves, but about their procedures respectively.

Journey is the game which you play each single day in that uncertain gamble whereas the destination is finally the reward which you'd been longing for so long!

Now, why journey is more important than the destination because the foremost fact is without it we cannot have a destination at all! Also, while you're in the journey, you discover yourself and you might read numerous quotes, several answers of getting a purpose and finding your true self.....but do you actually do that?

Ask better yourself!! So journey makes us explore the hidden talents and pushes us to the extremities of our own capability. Journey makes us realise what we did wrong in our practice that we failed. Also, in journey you're ALONE, mind this fact, everyone related to you, be it your family, friends or whom you consider your special one, all are just a part but maybe not involved. It's a fight till the death, which might take your last breath, but only you're there to tell yourself that "that it'll be fine,it's just a matter of time."

Hence being myself in a journey, I really don't know if I'm correct in answering this, but all I can tell is the experimental experience!!! It's just not motivation, it's the driving force which would guide you through the darkness! Assuming that *journey* is *process* and *destination* is the *result.* Frankly speaking, the quote is so relevant to my life or even most people's life on earth. I will explain the broad overview since I think story-telling will be too wordy. We live in a world that is constantly telling us to hurry up and achieve our goals as quickly as possible. We are told that the destination is all that matters, and that the journey is simply a means to an end. But what if we've been looking at things all wrong? What if the journey is actually more meaningful than the destination?

Think about it this way: you're planning a cross-country road trip. Would you rather drive straight through from point A to point B without stopping? Or would you prefer to take your time and enjoy the journey? Chances are, you would choose the latter. I would for sure. Why? Because the journey is where all the fun is! It's where you'll make memories and have experiences that you'll never forget. And it's not just road trips — the same principle applies to all aspects of life. So often, we get so focused on achieving our goals that we forget to enjoy the process. We become so obsessed with the destination that we forget to appreciate the journey. But life is not a race to the finish line. It's a journey to be savored and enjoyed, not rushed through.

The next time you find yourself getting caught up in the rat race of life, take a step back and try to enjoy the journey. Don't focus on getting to the destination as quickly as possible — focus on enjoying every step along the way. After all, isn't that what life is all about? The core truth was that we learned many things during our *process* in achieving our life goals *(result)* instead of when we got the result. In the *journey/process* stage, there were so many obstacles we'd been through and they already made us stronger, experienced, wiser, or even smarter. Meanwhile, the *result*, whether it was successful or failed, was influenced by how well we handled the journey. We cannot truly predict the result since everything is unpredictable. However, we can do and give our best effort to maximize the valuable outcomes from the journey/process. Finally, we'll always be grateful for the *result* we've made since we've leaned and trained from both the *journey* and the *result.* Sadly, in certain condition like educational, social, or working environment, *result/destination* tends to be more important than the *journey/process.* Most people appreciate us for the *result/destination* we've gained, not the *process/journey* we've been through.

Speaking for myself, I have to say this is what struck me when we first met this incredible business and learnt of how they started out, and what their purpose is. It was like meeting people you instantly felt you had known your whole life. Curiosity about what made us different and where we were similar was such an important part of discovering why this acquisition made sense to us all.

IV

THE DEATH OF SELF

There is a form of enlightenment where you are in a realized state while going about your ordinary, day-to-day life. It's less a matter of a one-time, "death of the self", and more of a realization that the self was never existing in the first place. And realizing that, resting in Being.

I think this question, and the subtext, "Can an enlightened person have dreams and set goals or everything loses its importance once that you reach the enlightenment?" speaks more about the underlying existential anxiety the person who asks this has. There is nothing wrong with that, and in fact, I have heard this question asked in different forms by different people. I've wondered about this myself too.

Put it in a different way, one of my teachers had said, "Things seem important because your 'self' wants it to be important." The very craving to elevate goals, and dreams and aspirations drives that kind of anxiety. If you tune into the feeling and really look at it, you might find that the anxiety is stemming from this fear that... losing these aspiration will mean a death of the self :-) In terms of practice, instead of wondering about this, and what enlightened people "are like", or what they "are allowed to do", tune into what you are feeling now, where the impulse to ask this question is arising in your body, and really just be with that feeling. Where is that expectation that enlightened people behave a certain way is arising from? Where is that wanting to know what is permissible action for an enlightened person is arising from?

The Death of Self: A Journey Through Lost Identity

As a young person, we are constantly in the process of discovering who we are. The world around us, with its fast pace and ever-changing expectations, seems to shape our sense of identity every day. But in the midst of this journey, there is an unsettling idea that we may lose ourselves, or experience what some call the "death of self."

The "death of self" is not a literal death, but rather a metaphorical one, a concept where we lose our true essence in the face of societal pressures, personal struggles, or self-doubt. It is the moment when we let go of the parts of ourselves that make us unique or special, just to fit into what others expect us to be.

One major factor in this process is the influence of social media. Platforms like Instagram, TikTok, and Snapchat bombard us with images of perfect lives, flawless appearances, and successful careers. It becomes easy to lose ourselves while trying to emulate others. We may start to believe that our worth depends on the number of likes we get or the number of followers we have, causing us to conform to trends and lose sight of our authentic selves.

Similarly, the expectations from school, family, and friends can create a pressure to be a certain way. The desire to succeed academically, fit in socially, or meet the standards set by loved ones can often make us forget who we are at the core. We may feel like we are constantly living up to others' dreams instead of pursuing our own.

But the death of self is not a permanent state. It's something that can be reversed. To revive our sense of self, we must reflect on our values, passions, and experiences. It requires us to be brave enough to break free from the molds that others have placed around us. Embracing imperfections, celebrating our individuality, and accepting that it's okay to not have everything figured out are all part of reclaiming our true identity. Ultimately, the death of self is a reminder that we must constantly fight to preserve who we are, no matter how loud the outside world gets. It is a journey of self-awareness, growth, and resilience, where we choose to be our most authentic selves, regardless of the pressures around us.

The Death of Self: An Exploration of Identity and Transformation

The concept of "the death of self" is an intriguing and thought-provoking topic that spans across various disciplines, including philosophy, psychology, spirituality, and even literature. It suggests a fundamental transformation of one's identity, often leading to the dissolution or complete shift of the ego, and can signify the end of the old self in pursuit of a new understanding of life and existence.

In spiritual and philosophical traditions, the "death of self" is sometimes viewed as a form of transcendence—letting go of the ego and material attachments to connect with a higher consciousness or universal truth. This form of "death" is not physical but rather psychological and emotional, where the individual sheds preconceived notions of identity, past experiences, and desires that form their sense of self. It is seen in many mystical practices, such as Buddhism, where the concept of anatman (no-self) emphasizes that the self is an illusion. In psychology, particularly in the context of personal growth, the death of self can refer to the process of overcoming old patterns of behavior and thinking. It involves confronting one's false beliefs, toxic self-images, and outdated constructs of the self. Through this process of self-dissolution, individuals can experience profound personal growth, resulting in a rebirth of the self with a clearer, more authentic identity. This often requires intense introspection and sometimes painful emotional work.

In literature, the theme of self-death is portrayed as a journey of self-discovery or a crisis of identity. Characters often undergo symbolic death experiences where they are forced to redefine who they are, which can result in personal renewal or existential despair. It is a recurring theme in works of existentialist authors like Albert Camus and Franz Kafka, who explore the alienation and isolation that accompany the loss of a coherent, fixed sense of self. Ultimately, the death of self is not a literal demise but a metaphorical concept tied to growth, transformation, and the pursuit of authenticity. It raises questions about what it truly means to be "yourself" and whether that self is something permanent or fluid. Does shedding the ego open a path to enlightenment and liberation, or does it risk leaving us lost in an existential void?

This topic invites deep contemplation on the nature of self, the ego, and the potential for profound shifts in consciousness that lead to the death of one identity and the birth of another.

The Death of Self: Losing Who You Are

As a teenager, there's a lot going on around you. The pressure to fit in, the expectations from your family and teachers, and the constant comparisons to others on social media can sometimes feel overwhelming. It's easy to get lost in it all. Sometimes, it feels like you're losing yourself in the process of trying to meet everyone else's standards. That's what I'd call the "death of self" — when you stop being true to who you really are and start living based on what everyone else wants you to be.

The idea of the "death of self" isn't about actually dying. It's about losing your sense of identity, becoming someone you're not, and letting go of the things that truly matter to you. It's when you stop doing things that make you happy or passionate and start trying to be someone you think others expect you to be. Maybe you stop expressing your opinions, give up on your dreams, or change your style just to fit in. It's like you become a version of yourself that doesn't feel real anymore. Social media plays a big part in this. Everyone's posting about their perfect lives, their vacations, their friendships, and their achievements. It can make you feel like you're not good enough or that you need to be like everyone else to get noticed or appreciated. Instead of being your true self, you start posting things that will get likes and comments, not because they're meaningful to you, but because you think they'll make others think you're cool or successful. At school, the pressure to be perfect can be just as bad. You might feel like you have to act a certain way to be popular, or maybe you feel like you have to excel in every subject to get into a good college. You might hide your real feelings, pretend you're okay when you're not, or even put on a mask to avoid being judged. Over time, this takes a toll on your self-worth and confidence. You stop trusting your own thoughts and feelings because you're always focused on what others think.

But it doesn't have to stay like this. The death of self isn't permanent. It's something you can fight back against. Rediscovering who you are is about being brave enough to stand up for yourself and what you believe in. It's about doing things that make you happy, even if they don't always fit in with what everyone else is doing. It's about saying no when something doesn't feel right and being honest about what you want out of life.

The key to bringing yourself back to life is authenticity. Embrace what makes you different, and don't be afraid to stand out. Learn to trust your gut, follow your passion, and don't let anyone else define who you should be. The "death of self" doesn't have to happen — you're in control of keeping the real you alive, no matter how hard it may seem sometimes.

The Death of Self: A Silent Struggle of Adulthood

As we move through life, adulthood brings with it a constant balancing act. We face responsibilities, career pressures, family obligations, and the expectations of society. For many of us, this daily grind can result in what can be called the "death of self"—a slow, often unnoticed process where the person we once were begins to fade away.

The "death of self" in adulthood is not a dramatic event but rather a quiet erosion of our sense of individuality and authenticity. It often begins with small compromises: putting your desires and dreams aside for the sake of others, conforming to what is expected in the workplace, or sacrificing personal passions for the stability of family life. Over time, these compromises accumulate, and you begin to lose touch with who you truly are beneath the roles you play. One of the main contributors to this loss is the pressure to succeed. As adults, we are often defined by our careers, the money we earn, the house we own, or the social status we've achieved. We push ourselves to meet these external measures of success, sometimes at the cost of our internal sense of fulfillment. We might give up hobbies we once loved, cut back on self-care, or even ignore our emotional needs because we believe these things aren't as important as meeting the demands of work or family. This results in a life where we are constantly giving to others but not replenishing our own sense of self.

Another factor in the death of self is the role that societal expectations play. In many cultures, there are strict ideas about what adulthood should look like—becoming a responsible, stable, and predictable person. While these are not inherently bad goals, they often lead to a life that is constrained by others' definitions of success. The idea of "fitting in" or conforming to societal norms can create a disconnect between what we truly value and what we feel obligated to do.

Moreover, the exhaustion of daily life can wear away at the essence of who we are. Many adults are so caught up in the demands of work, maintaining relationships, and managing finances that there is little time left for self-reflection or personal growth. This constant busyness can lead to a state of autopilot living, where we go through the motions of life without ever checking in with ourselves. It becomes easy to forget what once brought us joy or to dismiss what truly makes us happy.

However, the death of self doesn't need to be inevitable. It can be reversed, but it requires conscious effort and self-awareness. Rediscovering who you are in adulthood means taking the time to reflect on your values, your passions, and your boundaries. It's about finding moments of stillness amidst the chaos to reconnect with your true self. It means reassessing what success really looks like for you—not just through the lens of external expectations, but from the inside out.

Reviving the self may involve making space for personal interests again, even if it's as simple as reading a book for pleasure or taking a solo walk. It can mean having the courage to say no to things that drain you and protecting your mental and emotional well-being. It may require setting boundaries in relationships and work, allowing yourself the freedom to exist beyond the roles you've adopted.

Ultimately, the death of self is a reminder of the importance of self-awareness and authenticity. In a world that constantly demands more of us, it's easy to lose sight of who we are. But reclaiming our sense of self is a necessary act of self-preservation, ensuring that we live a life that feels true to who we are, not just to who the world expects us to be.

V

<u>Life as a continuous journey without a specific destination</u>

"In the absence of purpose, life is a journey that, when lived totally and authentically in a meditative state of awareness according to one's innate nature, MAY (not necessarily WILL) culminate with the discovery of one's hidden life purpose or destiny". If you care to check around, you may find that except for a small minority of highly talented people or geniuses, the majority of people started their lives without definite or clear-cut purposes. I for one won't dare to claim that I had started with one.

However, I have many sub-purposes, the first was to study as hard as I possibly could so that I could get the required qualifications for a decent occupation and a decent living - this could be called the sub-purpose for survival.

(Being the eldest child in a middle class family , I had to find a decent job and I am also doing one. I luckily landed myself with a teaching profession. For the next few years, I practised self-deprivation or delayed gratification (sacrificing my night life and weekends) by focusing my time and attention on my private studies I also want to clear some government exams of my profession.

My second sub-purpose was to become a best ever writer if I'll get chance to do so in my life I don't know where my destiny will take me but I want to do whatever I love to do after that I want to got married and started to build a family - this could be called the sub-purpose of propagation, to perform my duty of sustaining human species on earth .

Right now I can imagine this much only but as I learn from my uncle who is a civil servant tell me that.

My third sub-purpose happened at age 45. It dawned on me then that in the next ten years I would have to go for my mandatory retirement as a teacher. The spectre of retiring at the robust age of 55 without any marketability scared me.

Luck was on my side then. At that moment, the Government introduced a new policy allowing civil servants to opt for early retirement at age 45 onwards with the entitlement of half pension monthly payment calculated based on the last earned monthly salary. I exercised my option and joined a local public-listed corporation which allowed its senior executives to work up to 60 years of age or above.

To further equip myself, I started to read books on personal development (financial management, relationships and mind empowerment).From personal development, I developed interest in the New Age literature, followed by things mystical - this became my fourth sub-purpose, the beginning of my spiritual journey. If At age 54, I decided that I had had enough of working for others, and that it was time for me to do something for myself. However, my boss won't accept my request for leaving.

We worked out a compromised solution whereby I would be allowed to take two days off per week to read law (my childhood ambition) as an external student. I obtained my LLB (London U) three years later, at age 57 - this could be considered my fifth sub-purpose, that is the fulfillment of my childhood ambition. By then, my boss was due for retirement and we retired together. I then went into network marketing business where my law degree became very useful. Surprisingly, I made more money in my five-year network marketing business than my entire period of working for others -this could be considered my sixth sub-purpose.I was forced to retire from active life at age 66 when I was rendered paralysed (cervical spondylosis) suddenly without warning. After two major operations, I regained my mobility (with the support of cluthches) though the numbness and stiffness of my limbs remain until today.

I took what happened to me as a "blessing in disguise", that the Universe was testing me for my spiritual growth. As it turned out, my spiritual knowledge and understanding were put to test. I was found wanting. I quickly realised that understanding and experiencing were two totally different things. I started practising what I had learned in the past 15 years. I re-read what I had read in the past to increase my inner-knowing - this time around I did it with greater awareness. I have no qualms in saying that my spiritual journey has been made more meaningful from the very moment I was paralysed - this could be considered my seventh sub-purpose.

My only aim of narrating this ordinary life experience is none other than to show that when I started my life journey as a poor boy, I had had no idea whatsoever as to how it would evolve.

However, I have this instinctive feeling that if I kept learning and growing, ultimately my life purpose or destiny will be revealed to me - I need not do too much planning; what I need to do is to live my life very moment, totally, authentically, naturally (in accordance with my innate nature) and consciously, and my life's sub-purposes and ultimate purpose will be revealed to me as time moves on. Now, at age 77, with my understanding and experiences, I dare say that in general the ultimate purpose of life is to grow to the fullest, both outwardly and inwardly. As to what "the fullest" means, it will depend on how fully, authentically, naturally and consciously we live our lives.

Based on this, I would say that my ultimate purpose is to spread the message of godliness and love, unconditional love.

It's a journey with some expected & unexpected destinations. Let me explain it you.

Suppose you want to achieve some goals or dreams or fulfill your bucket list & you got some then it will be the expected result. But when life surprises you with different things like health problems(mental & physical) , people , some twisted turns , heartbreaks , shattered dreams & many more - these are the times when the destination or result is not what you wanted & if you talk about death can be the ultimatum ,then my friend i have a reminder here. you can't feel the journey here cause you are not even alive then. Death is the universal truth . It's not the destination where you & me are going .We are born to be the eyewitness of life. So make it yours ,uniquely . It has to have the word " enjoy" to live each & every moment doesn't matter how good or bad the destinations are! The train will start to run again & trust me , this station too shall pass.

Life as a Continuous Journey Without a Specific Destination

Life is often thought of as a destination—something we must reach, a goal to accomplish, or a dream to fulfill. From childhood, we are taught that success lies in the achievements we make along the way: a diploma, a job, a family, or a certain level of financial or social status. Yet, if we step back and reflect more deeply, it becomes clear that life is not so much about reaching a specific destination, but about the journey itself, an ongoing experience where the process of living becomes more important than any fixed end point.

Viewing life as a continuous journey without a specific destination changes how we engage with it. This perspective invites us to embrace uncertainty, spontaneity, and growth. It encourages us to move away from the idea that life's value comes from reaching a particular stage or milestone and to instead focus on the lessons, relationships, and experiences we gain along the way.

One of the most profound ways that life is like a journey is in its ever-changing nature. At any given moment, our path can shift in unexpected directions—sometimes gently, sometimes abruptly. The pursuit of a particular goal may not unfold the way we imagined, or we might find that our desires evolve as we grow older. For instance, what we dreamed of in our teenage years may no longer align with our priorities in adulthood. We may start down one career path only to discover a different field of work that brings us greater fulfillment. The realization that life's meaning lies in the journey rather than a fixed destination frees us from the anxiety of rigid expectations and allows us to flow with life's natural rhythms.

Another aspect of life as a continuous journey is the importance of self-discovery. Every step along the way offers opportunities to learn about who we are, what we value, and how we relate to the world around us. It's not just about achieving external success, but about evolving internally. We are constantly changing, shaped by experiences, relationships, and challenges. Each phase of life offers new lessons that contribute to our personal growth. In the same way a traveler might discover new landscapes, we too discover new facets of ourselves as we move forward in life. These discoveries make the journey worth taking, as they enrich our understanding of what it means to be human.

Life's journey also brings us into contact with others, and it is through our relationships that we often find meaning. The people we meet along the way— family, friends, colleagues, strangers—serve as companions on our path. These connections shape our journey, sometimes guiding us, sometimes challenging us. The relationships we form are often more valuable than any material success we may achieve, as they offer love, understanding, and companionship. Just as a traveler learns from fellow travelers, we learn from the people we meet, and in turn, we contribute to their journeys as well.

Moreover, the process of living is filled with joy, sorrow, triumph, and loss. These moments, whether they are difficult or joyous, shape the path we travel. The peaks of happiness offer us moments of reflection, while the valleys of sorrow teach us resilience and empathy. Understanding that life is not about avoiding hardship but about learning from it makes us more capable of navigating the unpredictable nature of the journey. In this sense, life's value lies in the richness of each moment, not in the assurance of a particular outcome.

It's also essential to recognize that the absence of a fixed destination allows for the freedom of exploration. Life as an open-ended journey invites creativity, curiosity, and a willingness to try new things. Without the pressure of arriving at a specific place, we are free to explore different passions, experiment with new ideas, and make mistakes along the way. This freedom is a gift, offering us the chance to redefine what success means on our own terms. It's not about reaching the top of a mountain, but about enjoying the climb and finding joy in every twist and turn of the road.

In essence, life as a continuous journey without a specific destination is about embracing the adventure of living itself. It encourages us to let go of the need for certainty and control and to accept the inherent uncertainty of life. By focusing on the present moment and the experiences we gain along the way, we can appreciate the beauty and complexity of the journey, knowing that it is the path, not the end, that defines us. Life may not have a single, final destination, but it offers countless opportunities for discovery, growth, and meaning as we move forward, step by step, embracing the journey for what it is.

Life as a Continuous Journey Without a Specific Destination

As we navigate through adulthood, we often find ourselves caught in the pursuit of specific goals—career achievements, financial stability, personal success, or societal validation. We are conditioned to think that life's worth lies in reaching defined milestones, and that once we achieve a certain level of success, happiness will naturally follow. However, over time, it becomes increasingly clear that life is not a destination to be reached, but a continuous journey without a specific endpoint. This shift in perspective can be both liberating and transformative, offering us the freedom to live fully in the present rather than focusing solely on some distant future achievement.

The idea of life as an endless journey, rather than a fixed destination, challenges the conventional notion that life's value is tied to specific accomplishments. From a young age, we are taught to work toward goals—graduate from school, get a good job, buy a house, and perhaps start a family. These are natural milestones, but when we place all our focus on them, we risk missing the richness of the everyday experience. In reality, the journey of life is far more nuanced, and its beauty lies in the twists and turns along the way. The moments of joy, the challenges we face, and the relationships we build are what truly shape our lives.

When we view life as a journey, we are better able to embrace the uncertainty and unpredictability that comes with it. As adults, we often try to control the direction of our lives, thinking that achieving certain goals will bring us peace or fulfillment. But life doesn't always follow a linear path. There are unforeseen detours, unexpected opportunities, and sometimes even setbacks that challenge our course. These interruptions are not failures—they are part of the journey. They help us grow, learn, and adjust our perspective. If life were merely about reaching a fixed destination, we would miss the chance to evolve through the unpredictable nature of existence.

One of the most profound aspects of seeing life as a journey is the understanding that we are always in the process of becoming. Adulthood, unlike childhood, doesn't offer a clear roadmap to follow. As we age, we accumulate experiences that redefine who we are. The person you were at 25 may not be the person you are at 45, and that's perfectly natural. Life doesn't have a predetermined destination; instead, it is an evolving narrative shaped by the choices we make and the lessons we learn along the way. Embracing this fluidity allows us to be more adaptable and open to the changes that come with different stages of life.

Living without the pressure of a specific destination also allows for greater self-acceptance. As adults, we are often our harshest critics, constantly measuring our success against societal expectations or comparing ourselves to others. We may feel that we have to achieve certain things by a particular age or that our lives should be neatly aligned with others' timelines. When we let go of the idea that life must lead to a particular outcome, we free ourselves from the stress of comparison. We begin to see the value in each step we take, regardless of whether it aligns with a predetermined idea of success. This acceptance helps us find contentment in the present moment, appreciating where we are, rather than where we think we should be.

Another powerful lesson in embracing life as a journey is that it encourages us to focus on the process, not the outcome. Much of adult life can feel like a series of tasks to be checked off—paying bills, working long hours, maintaining relationships, and managing responsibilities. Yet, when we view life as a journey, we begin to understand that the purpose of these daily activities is not to reach an end, but to engage fully with the experiences they bring. The relationships we build, the work we do, and the small joys we encounter each day are what make life meaningful. It's the conversations with a friend, the feeling of accomplishment after completing a project, or the quiet moments of reflection that matter, not just the end results.

The journey mindset also allows us to find meaning in adversity. Life is never free from hardship, and as adults, we face challenges that test our resilience—health issues, loss, professional struggles, and personal doubts. But if we view these struggles as part of the larger journey, we can gain strength from them. Every difficulty provides an opportunity to learn something new about ourselves and to refine our character. Rather than seeing obstacles as detours from our "destination," we begin to see them as integral to the process of becoming who we are meant to be.

Ultimately, embracing the idea of life as a continuous journey frees us from the burden of having to "arrive" at some final destination. It allows us to live authentically, to savor the richness of each moment, and to appreciate the depth of our experiences. Life's true value doesn't lie in reaching a particular goal or stage—it lies in how we move through life, how we grow, how we adapt, and how we relate to others along the way. By letting go of the notion that life has a specific endpoint, we allow ourselves the freedom to live fully and meaningfully in the present, knowing that the journey itself is where the real treasures are found.

VI

<u>Care Not To Care</u>

Letting go means to come to the realization that some people are a part of your history, but not a part of your destiny.   _SteveMaraboli

One of my friends told me this story to inspire me to move on. There lived a man, he wanted to climb the highest mountain in the world. After many years of preparation, he decided to give it a go. Because he wanted to achieve glory alone, he started climbing the mountain alone. It was cold, the night arrived, it was dark, zero visibility but he still wanted to climb. Instead of taking a halt, he kept climbing.

Suddenly, his foot slipped and he lost his control. It was a free fall; he felt the pull of gravity. In those moments of great fear, it reminded of all the good and bad things he did in his life. He was now thinking of how close was his death, all of a sudden, he felt a hard pull by a rope tied to his waist. His body was now hanging, with only a support of rope, He cried and screamed, *"Help me God."*. A voice came from cloud, *"What do you want me to do?"*

The man cried, *"Save me God!"*

The voice came, *"Will you do as I say?"*

The man cried, *"Yes anything, please save me."*

The voice came, *"Cut the rope tied on your waist."*

The man did not cut the rope and held it by all his strength. Next morning when the rescue team arrived, it said that the climber was dead and frozen, he was holding on his rope which was frozen,

Only six feet above ground!

So, how attached are you with your rope? Will you let go?

***To let come new and better things, let go of the old. ***

The important thing that you should always remember is that life is **uncertain** and **unfair.** There are times when we put sincere efforts into something but it just doesn't work out for us. But has life been designed to oblige our emotions? The answer is NO. So, what is the damn point of sulking over that 'life changing' exam or interview or offer or proposal or relationship or whatever that you might have lost? **Something that**

is unchangeable or uncontrollable can only be accepted. You don't have any other choice. If you accept it, you allow yourself to move on but if you don't accept it, you voluntarily unlock the door to hell on earth.And mind you, anybody who seems to be happy around you have either already battled or is going to battle their own demons in the near future. Nobody is blessed enough to have everything sorted in life. Things become ugly at least once in everybody's lifetime.

Don't hold on to misery because it's only going to make you more miserable. Worrying is anyways not going to solve your problem. You don't have to learn to let go of things, you just have to believe in the concept that you are still alive to make your life better again. You are still alive to try just one more time or give your best shot at something new altogether. Learning to let go is much harder than holding on. In the words of Ann Landers: "Some people believe holding on and hanging in there aresigns of great strength. However, there are times when it takes much more strength to know when to let go and then do it." Why do we cling onto past sorrows, bad relationships, old things, meaningless goals? Isn't our tendency to define ourselves through what we own rather than who we are hurting us in the long term? If only it was that easy. As human beings, we hold grudges, we attach sentimental meaning to inert objects, we like to revisit the pastand <u>worry about the future</u>. How can we learn to let go?

Let go of the past

All human beings have been emotionally hurt at some point in their lives. Our ability to feel pain is universal. However, research suggests that when emotions hinder our ability to heal from a painful event, it's an indication that we aren't moving forward in a growth-oriented way. Practicing emotionalagility is one of the most practical ways to let go of past experiences which are preventing you from moving on. It consists in:

- **Connection.** Talking it out with someone you feel safe around. Share your experience and your feelings. Don't keep it all bottled up.
- **Contribution.** The next stage is to help others who have gone through a similar experience. There is no right time for this stage, and for some people it may be never. Not all painful experiences need to turn into a contribution opportunity, but it can be helpful in some cases.
- **Compassion.** Be kind to yourself. Make sure you are making progress, but don't rush it. It's not a race. Journaling can help to explore your

inner world and make sure you approach your journey from a place of self-compassion.

Sometimes, you need to create physical distance. Staying in a place where something hurtful happened can keep on bringing the painful memory back.

Let go of the illusion of control

Many parents will experience the terrifying moment where they will need to let go of their kid, and let them explore the world on their own. It starts with their first step and only gets worse with time, until they leave for university or get their first job and move out of the house. Learning to let go of your control can be extremely difficult in this case. As Julie Lythcott-Haims, the former dean of freshmen at Stanford University, puts it: "Like every other mammal parent we need to raise offspring who can fend for themselves out in the world without us. Let's not lose sight of the fact that our job as parents is actually to put ourselves out of a job." But it's not the only area where we struggle to let go of control. Managers who micromanage their teams, people who keep grabbing control of the conversation, and those who stick to rigid rituals—these people are all after a sense of control. How can we let go? Beyond giving ourselves the <u>illusion of control</u>, we need to give controlto get control. In practice, it means giving people (your kid, youremployees, yourself) the flexibility to play with the rules. Instead of a rigidframework, define a <u>playground</u> with key principles. It works for conversations too. Instead of asking closed questions, ask open questions. While it may give you the feeling of losing control, you are still the one choosing which questions to ask, which is extremely powerful.

Let go of things

Mari Kondo built a huge empire around helping people to declutter their homes by letting go of their old stuff. Why do people find it so hard to let go of these physical things?Sometimes, it's because they have sentimental value. This sentimental value can stem from past experiences or future expectations. Objects with past sentimental value may include a souvenir from a holiday, a bracelet you were wearing on your first date, a cup your grandmother gave you. Objects with future sentimental value may be a box of craft supplies for when you will finally start learning how to paint, a collection of books about architecture you will definitely study at some point, or a set of kettlebells for when you will exercise at home—someday. Letting go of these feels like letting go of a dream.

Other times, it's because we are scared to be wasteful. Either we think we may need that thing again, or we feel guilty about the money we spent in the first place. This is the sunk cost fallacy rearing its ugly head. A great way to get rid of stuff is to do it progressively. Start with the easy stuff—items such as gadgets you haven't used in years, old papers without much sentimental value, or, the easiest of all, stuff you don't even remember what they are or what they're supposed to be used for. (most of us have tons of these in our houses) Gradually move up your decluttering work towards more sentimental items, asking yourself: "Why do I care about this item?" Very often, you will realise that the need behind your sentimental attachment to a particular item can be fulfilled in other ways, such as a gratitude practice or calling/visiting the person it makes you think of more often. (this also works to a certain extend for people you love who have passed away, visiting them physically or in your mind, which is called "inner wisdom imagery" by psychologists)

This should not be an extremely painful process. Learning to let go of things is mainly about questioning the actual value of your stuff and letting go of unnecessary things. If you do deeply care a lot about some items, keep them. Who cares how tidy your home is? As long as it feels comfortable, it really is all that matters.

Let go of people

It may sound harsh, but it is sometimes better to let go of certain relationships. Some people may belong to a past which doesn't reflect who you are today, other people may have changed in a way that has changed the relationship. Learning to let go of a relationship doesn't have to be negative, it can be an opportunity for personal growth. First, it's important to let yourself feel all the range of emotions the relationship brings about—the good and the bad. Most relationships we care about are complex. Take off your love or friendship goggles and embrace that complexity. Then, take time to reflect. What did you learn from this relationship—about the world, about yourself? Some people find it useful to write a letter. Whether you give/send it or not to the person, it may be helpful in articulating your thoughts and emotions. Finally, practice forgiveness. It may be that by going through this process you actually realise this relationship is worth keeping. And if that's not the case, gently let go, be grateful for the lessons you learned about the world and yourself, and keep the good memories as tokens of a relationship that helped you grow.

Learning to let go of things you can't control or change and accepting life as it is can be a challenging but ultimately rewarding process. Here are some strategies that may help:

    1. Practice mindfulness: Mindfulness techniques, such as meditation and deep breathing, can help you focus on the present moment and let go of worries about the past or future.

2. Focus on what you can control: Shift your focus toward the aspects of your life that you do have control over, such as your attitudes, behaviours, and choices.
3. Cultivate self-compassion: Treat yourself with kindness and understanding, especially in difficult moments. Remember that it's okay to feel the way you do.
4. Seek support: Talking to friends, family, or a therapist can provide valuable perspective and help you process your emotions.
5. Find meaning: Engage in activities that bring you joy and a sense of purpose. This can help shift your focus away from things you can't change.

Remember, learning to let go and accept life as it is takes time and practice, so be patient with yourself as you navigate this process.

Nobody likes to lose.

It feels like crap to see our efforts crumble. It sucks to be told on our face that we are not good enough (at least for now). But unfortunately, we DO need to lose sometimes. Losing is like a slap on the face. It works as an alarm clock, waking us up and bringing us back to reality. And we need that sometimes! We need to be reminded that there is always room for improvement and that we can always be better than we are today.

There are great benefits to losing. The reflection process that the losing puts us through is not experienced by the winner. The thorough inner search, replaying every single step of the way; every interaction, every conversation, trying to figure out where the weaknesses are, is something that the winner doesn't go through. We have 2 options whenever we are faced with defeat, we either drop the towel, lose face and fall into depression or pick up our bags and go back into training. The 1st choice would turn our fault into a failure, but the 2nd would turn it into a glorious comeback! I recently wrote about a couple of things that I have found common among winners. That past article actually made me start wondering about the least celebrated participants. What do they have in common? There is always only 1 winner, meaning that the majority are always losers, how about them? With the odds of winning against them, there has to be something among all of them.

Losing can be extremely rewarding.

Just as the saying goes, "we get what we need and not what we want." Or as Steve Jobs said "you can't connect the dots looking forward you can only connect them looking backwards." Now this will all depend on how the person deals with losing and which option they decide to take.

Losing makes you braver.

The majority of us don't even dare to participate. We are our own obstacle, filling our heads with millions of reasons that tell us why we should not pursue our goals. Nobody likes to lose and those who decided to join the chase for victory overcame it. They for sure hear their fears screaming in their heads but decide not to listen to them. This shows bravery and should also be recognised.

Losing allows you to grow.

Personally, mentally, physically. In order to overcome the shock of losing, a person must understand where the pitfall was. By doing this, the individual is able to identify the areas that need strengthening. By focusing on developing an overall, more complete individual, the former loser is able to outgrow him or herself. It's in your hands to decide what you do with your experiences. I personally don't believe in failure. I think that falling is human and it will happen to all of us at some point. But what matters is if we decide to learn from it or not. "When we meet real tragedy in life, we can react in 2 ways – either by losing hope and falling into self-destructive habits, or by using the challenge to find our inner strength" – Dalai Lama

In short:-

Life sends many opportunities our way, but it also sends difficulties, challenges, inequities and injustice.

It is not necessary that the world will come to our support. We must learn to go and move on.

VII

<u>Why are we the way we are ?</u>

Somewhere along the way, during my late 20s, I discovered I was bored with everything – my relationships, my career, my hobbies, even my writing.And then I came up with some punchy ways to fix and change that behavior, like toughen up, stop comparing myself to others, and just deal with it? I practiced these strategies for about a day and a half before realizing what a pile of crap it all was. I gave up trying to inspire myself and regressed to the comforting ease of boredom and being dispassionate.

Since then, I learned something pretty profound: You can't change yourself.I don't mean, you can't change your body weight or your hair color. I mean, you can't change your true identity. If you thought you were the "fat kid" when you were younger, you will always see yourself as the fat kid, even if you are a super skinny runway model. If you thought you were the attention-seeking middle child when you were a kid, then you will always feel like that person into adulthood, even if you end up with a boring desk job in marketing. These are traits in you that are with you forever, and no amount of self-help or plastic surgery will help you "change" that.

So now what? What does that mean, exactly?

Now, here's the crazy thing, that took me three days to finally figure out: Accept it. Accept everything. The good, the bad, the ugly. Accept that you are selfish sometimes. That you are judgmental. That you are weak. That you are strong. This doesn't mean you have to embrace everything. It simply means, you accept, then move on.

What makes people Happy?

People's day-to-day happiness and well-being depend far more on how they approach life than on what life brings.

Research suggests that 10% of happiness depends on our life circumstances, 50% on our genes and 40% on our behaviors.Unfortunately we focus most on the first factor which can only result in occasional short term happiness. The most important aspect to focus here is the last one-intentional behavior. People who are happy do things differently. One of them is to focus on intrinsic goals: goals that one feels are important to him/her achieve. Some goals are more intrinsically important to your well-being, meaning that they are pursued for their own sake rather than to get something else. Spending more time with your children or friends can be an intrinsic goal because you probably truly want to spend more time with them—not so that you can obtain some other goal.

More desirable than occasional episodes of happiness, is an overriding sense of contentment and pleasure- subjective well-being. That's what we should aim for.

Why we feel hurt?

We feel hurt when we perceive that the other person values our relationship less than what we want.There are 6 situations when we feel hurt Rejection,Being ignored,Criticism,Betrayal,Malicious teasing, Being taken for granted Scientists have found that when we're hurt emotionally, the neurotransmitters in the brain act the same way as when we're hurt physically. From an evolutionary standpoint, pain is nature's way to keep us from doing things that might hurt us. If we couldn't feel pain by cuts or burns, we wouldn't be careful around sharp objects or fire next time.

Similarly, emotional pain is nature's way of simulating us to work on our relationships. Making positive social circles and forming rewarding relationships are crucial to our well being. Feeling hurt at times only makes us act towards this goal.

What makes relationships succeed or fail?

Some extent of success of a relationship can be predicted just by personality of a person. By nature, if a person is disagreeable, hostile, suspicious, or selfish, then that person is likely to have   less satisfying relationships than a person who is agreeable, easy-going, trusting and giving.

Remaining depends on how well personalities of two people mesh with each other.

The lecture mentions a very interesting theory called **Interdependence theory.**

A relationship is a combination of rewards a person gets and costs (s)he incurs. Outcome of a relationship is the reward minus the effort.

Now you might think that relationships where net outcome is positive (profit) would be successful and failure for negative outcome (loss). But no, this is where Interdependence Theory comes into play. According to Interdependence Theory, we all have a benchmark for judging whether we're making enough profit or not. Generally this comparison is determined by our past experiences of relationships. Now, a person feels satisfied in a relationship only when the net outcome is more than their comparison level.

People can be unhappy in a relationship that from an outsider's perspective would appear to be rewarding because their positive outcomes fall below their comparison level. They're not making as much of a profit as they'd like.

Why are we the way we are? Is it desire, compulsion or destiny?

Every person is unique. We are all exclusive, little parts of this huge universe. We are crafted beautifully and are connoisseur of our own special art and talent.

Is it desire? No one *desires* to be the way they are. They just have innate traits. Can we be successful by desire? Yes. Can we be emotional by desire? No, we cannot; because that's our basic quality.

Is it compulsion? No, it's not. It's just the way we are born. Someone's an epicure; someone else is an odd-ball. It's all traits-just the way we are born. We can only be compulsive for those traits which we learn over time. Cleanliness Disorder can be compulsive.

Is it destiny, then? Kind of. I am a true believer of fate and karma. Even while we remain unaware, karma cycles on. It goes from one birth to another to another to yet another. This is a vicious cycle. The way one person is and the way we suffer, is all connected to our karma. So in a way, it could be destiny. We may be at crossroads of meddling fate with someone.

And in the words of Rajesh Khanna, "Babu Moshai, ye duniya ek rangmanch hai aur hum rangmanch ki kathputliyan."

We are truly generated, operated and destroyed by one supreme power; and that is why, we are the way He wants and the way we are!
Free will and destiny are two sides of the same coin. One doesn't exist without the other.

If the behaviour of human beings is predestined, it is destined as per the will of some entity or the other. The parents choose how a child should behave. The teachers choose how the students should behave. We choose how we should behave and subconsciously train ourselves to behave that way (habit forming — like brushing your teeth, cracking a sarcastic joke, lighting a cigarette) under specific circumstances.

If this universal design allows us to use our will actively, the will can only conceive ideas based on what the mind already knows, based on prior knowledge or memory.

From this perspective, compulsion and destiny arise from the concept of desire: If we want something, it is because we have prior associations in our mind that we would like to live or relive. If we do something because we feel we have to, we would operate merely on instinct; altruism would not exist. If we behaved because we were coded that way, we would not have the capacity to imagine. To the question on why are we here... this is something that can never be answered by anyone in words, there are people who know the reason behind existence but that has to be experienced and not spoken in words - the answer to this is not something that can be understood by intelligence, but it can only be felt by heart... even if someone tells you the reason of being here your nature will still question it further and the loop shall continue till you give up the question itself... and the giving up happens very soon because of our inherent configuration of not to ponder on such topic. Well personally I believe that we all just see what we want to. And we are nothing but objects of our own projected self consciousness and desire. In unfamiliar spaces we pretend to be what we want to be and slowly the pretence gives away to believing that it is what we are. I reject the concept of free will because nothing I do can ever be of any significance in the grand scheme of things but at the same time I reject destiny because I think that there is still some significance to my deeds and thoughts. I lean away from destiny tho and more towards free will.

Compulsion was a total wild card option for me. Sure we might be COMPELLED to be and behave a certain way but that doesnt change what/who we are... even though we might internalize it in the process and it might become us in more ways we could imagine.

So yeah, as I write this answer, I figure that there truly is only one thing that really makes us what we are. That is desire. What we desire to be and what others desire us to be (compulsion), and in the tussle between them, somewhere.... we shape ourselves Its evolution. If you're talking about the behavior of our species as a whole, evolution is responsible for that. Think of it as, certain algorithms being coded in our genes just the way we do in computer. These genetically coded programs tells us how to act in different situations which maximise our chance of survival or producing one's own copy. This is the reason why we can find some behavior common in our species with other species because we are have evolved from them with better traits, which makes are survival more probable. It can't be desire. Things never come out the way we want it, does it?

Is it a compulsion? Maybe. Many times we are forced to do things we don't want or take decisions we are not comfortable with. But then again we are free to choose our own course of action, which is true for most people.

It's karma then. But what if someone has never had a chance? Someone with a disability or someone confined in a prison can't always choose their own destiny, right?

It is fate. It is a combination of our choices, privileges, past actions and limitations. We still choose our destiny, as long as we are free to act and take decisions.
We are what others are, it might sound paradoxical but its inevitably true that we are what the people

around us are and so are the people around them. I think the difference arises, when a situation around a person differs be it among siblings friends or partners, I always wondered why some are good and others are bad and why would Allah choose who he wants to be good and bad, do we lose the choice of our way of life, and way of life I mean not jewels luxury comfort.... What I meant was the way we treat others the way we treat ourselves our soul the people around us.

Now little later when I was exposed to the drop of ocen of life from the arms of my parents I then knew everyone is good and bad in someone's story and the more good stories you make the more good you are, but how to make such good stories here is where destiny plays its cards some of us might deny about the existence of destiny and argue the we are open to our choices but just take a deep breath guys and think of the past incidents in your life haven't we all faced such a moment when we chose be something but turn out to be other, our choice are merely a illusion which leads to the full stop of our mere lives. we all are meant to live our life but sometimes we choose to live a way of life and here's when we loose peace we start making bad stories in other life we are harming our beautiful soul we become something we were never before, it is inevitable to escape our destination but the path we choose for is all we have in this life

We are the way we are because we guide ourselves by the behavior of our eco system. We were born without our knowledge. We grow up and understand our surroundings, our family background, economic status, etc. We learn lessons in life through school and our experiences. These experiences make us behave the way we behave. In a way it is a compulsion based on destiny. We also die without our planning just the way we were born without our planning.
Definitely, it's not desire.

Compulsion, may be. Some situations in our life compel us to acquire certain traits and characters. The situations around us, the environment ,surroundings, the country we stay in, the family we live in, etc... determine the way we are, our character ,traits ,personality, our actions and behaviours.

Our destiny is also a reason for this. But it is upto us ,if we want to embrace it or not. Destiny gives us choices sometimes. We should decide which choice might change our lives and improve us. And which is not.

VIII

Kehna Karna Nibhna – The Art of Saying What You Don't Mean and Doing Less

"Kehna karna nimbhana—oh, absolutely! It's all about making grand promises you have zero intention of keeping, and then pretending like it never happened. After all, who needs consistency when you've got a mouth full of empty words, right? The real charm is in saying all the right things and then conveniently forgetting them when it's time to act. Commitment? That's for people who have nothing better to do with their time." This could be a playful way to highlight the irony of empty words while poking fun at the idea of commitment. Would this tone work for the context you're thinking about?

Picture this: You've just met a friend at a coffee shop. After the usual pleasantries—"How's life? Oh, I've been so busy!"—they hit you with the classic line, "I swear, I'm going to start going to the gym. This time for real!" You know the drill. The gym membership will be used exactly once (to take that first Instagram photo) and then the gym bag will end up gathering dust in the corner, a sad reminder of empty promises.

But hey, who needs action when you've got words that sound really convincing, right? Ah, **kehna karna nibhna**—the classic trick of pretending to be a person of principle while you're secretly the master of contradiction. Who doesn't love the elegance of someone confidently spouting out promises, only to immediately follow up with the grace of a toddler trying to walk? It's truly an art form. The trick is simple: say something, act like it matters, and when it's time to deliver, just... don't. Why bother with the hassle of actually following through when empty words are so much easier?

Promises Made, Promises Broken

Let's dive into the magic behind it. You make a promise, usually with great flair, sometimes even with a sincere tone. You might even sprinkle in a few dramatic pauses to really sell the idea that this time, you mean it. Everyone believes you. They might even buy you a gift or say something like, "You're so dependable." But deep down, you know the real plan: say what needs to be said, and then... just don't show up. Why would you? The beauty of "kehna karna" is in the effortless performance of the first half. Actually doing something, now that's boring. Here's the thing: Promising is easy. It's like making a wish on a shooting star—except you're not even looking up, and the star is probably just a passing airplane. But still, people are impressed! The beauty of saying "I'll do it!" is that you don't even have to specify when. You can always push that deadline to a time that's "just around the corner"... which, surprise, turns out to be perpetually around the corner. Want to start a new project? Just tell everyone you'll begin next week. When next week rolls around, well, there's always the following week. It's a masterpiece of procrastination. And you, my friend, are the Picasso of postponing.

The Power of "Later"

One of the most charming tools in the "kehna karna nibhna" toolkit is the strategic use of "later." You don't need to actually do anything now; just give it time. Tell people, "I'll get to it later," and then forget—preferably in a way that makes it their fault for reminding you. After all, when you said you'd do it, who could have known you meant "later" in the most vague and uncommitted sense possible? It's a magical get-out-of-jail card. Your job? Say it with confidence, and the "doing" part can stay locked in the safe.

The Art of Distraction – "Look Over There!"

While your audience is still pondering how you managed to pull off the "kehna karna" stunt, it's time to give them something else to focus on. This could be a new promise, a half-hearted apology, or even a vague comment about how "life just gets in the way." The key is to distract them long enough that they forget the first promise you made—because let's face it, who remembers the last thing someone said when they've already started saying something else?

The Fine Line Between Sarcasm and Truth

Now, let's take a moment to address the delicate balance here. When you promise someone the moon and stars and then don't deliver, there's a fine line between sarcasm and truth. Sarcasm makes the bitter pill of non-commitment easier to swallow. It's all part of the performance. "Oh, I meant to get that done," you'll say, rolling your eyes, as if it's everyone else's fault for believing that you'd actually follow through. Ah, but the truth is—sarcasm is the perfect shield. When you say something with just enough mockery, no one expects you to do it anyway. You've created your own invisible forcefield of zero responsibility.

Who Needs Consistency Anyway?

In the world of **kehna karna nibhna**, consistency is an overrated concept. Why bother being consistent when you can be selectively unreliable? Why honor your commitments when there's no fun in actually doing the work? Sure, consistency takes time and effort—things that are much better spent on posting motivational quotes and keeping up appearances. The true beauty of non-delivery lies in its unpredictability. Will they actually show up this time? Who knows? The suspense is half the fun. You get to keep everyone on their toes, all while avoiding the mundane task of following through.

The Power of 'Later' (a.k.a. The Secret Weapon)

"Later" is the ultimate get-out-of-jail card. It's the word that sounds so promising and full of possibility, but in reality, it's a trap. If you say it enough times, you can get away with anything. Forget to help someone move? "Oh, I'll come by later!" Want to avoid that awkward conversation? "We can talk later!"

The key is to make "later" sound so sincere and full of intention, that it almost sounds like a solid plan. But, surprise! The "later" you promised never actually arrives, because "later" is a mythical land where nothing ever gets done, and the inhabitants are all experts at procrastination.

The Fine Art of Saying What Sounds Good

Here's the truth: we all know how to say the right thing at the right time. Words flow like a smooth jazz melody, and suddenly, you're the person everyone turns to for motivation and advice. "I'll definitely help you with that project," you declare, your voice full of enthusiasm, the embodiment of support. But inside, you're already calculating how to escape the responsibility without looking like a total flake.

The trick is simple: make the promise sound so irresistible, so absolutely convincing, that people forget to ask for actual results. You've mastered the art of looking committed, while quietly slipping into the shadows when it's time to act. Bravo.

"Consistency Is for the Birds"

Consistency is highly overrated. Why be consistently reliable when you can be **sporadically inspiring**? The beauty of **kehna karna nibhna** is in the thrill of unpredictability. Will they follow through? Who knows? That's what makes it exciting!

You don't want to be predictable. Who wants to be known as the dependable person who does exactly what they said they'd do? Yawn. Instead, aim for a mysterious aura of unreliability. One minute you're promising the world, and the next minute, you're nowhere to be found. You're like an unpredictable hero in a rom-com—except the "romantic" part is missing and you're never actually coming back to fix the situation.

Distraction: The Masterstroke of Evading Accountability

If there's one thing that makes **kehna karna nibhna** so fun, it's the ability to distract people when things get awkward. You can't show up to a meeting you promised you'd attend? No problem. Just pull out the big guns—"Sorry, I got caught up in something urgent! But hey, let's plan another time!"—and then immediately steer the conversation into something completely irrelevant, like the weather or the latest celebrity gossip.

It's a beautiful sleight of hand, really. Just keep them talking about anything other than the fact that you didn't do what you said you'd do. You'll have them questioning whether they even wanted you there in the first place. Problem solved.

The Sincerity of Insincerity

Here's the trick no one tells you: If you sound genuinely sorry, they'll forgive you every time. It's called the "Sincerity Card." You've seen it in action. You've used it yourself. You make eye contact, you nod thoughtfully, and you say, "I know, I know, I really should have done this." Then, bam! You've established that you're not a terrible person. You're just someone who meant well but never quite got around to it.

And guess what? Most people will let you off the hook. It's almost like they don't want to be the person who holds you accountable, because that's uncomfortable. So, you'll waltz away scot-free, feeling like a charmer, while secretly avoiding the work you promised.

So, let's give a round of applause to the masters of **kehna karna nibhna**—the ones who talk big but do little. The ones who promise the world and hand over an empty box instead. They've perfected the art of words over action, and frankly, that's all they need to keep the game going. After all, who needs delivery when you've got a talent for delivering only what people want to hear? It's the gift that keeps on giving, even if the recipient's left wondering where it went. So, there you have it: the magical, hilarious, and totally charming art of **kehna karna nibhna**. You don't need to actually do anything to be seen as reliable or trustworthy. You just need to be good at making grand promises, using a lot of words that sound meaningful, and getting away with doing absolutely nothing.

Remember, folks, consistency is overrated. Action? Pfft, who needs that when you've got the power of words and distractions at your disposal? Just say it with confidence, and the rest will take care of itself— or, more accurately, not take care of itself, but who's keeping track?

Key Takeaways:

- **Talk big** and say all the right things.
- Use the magic word "later" as often as possible.
- Distraction is your best friend.
- Remember, sarcasm is a shield. You're not really serious about anything, are you?
- Consistency? Overrated. Excitement lies in the unexpected non-delivery.

IX

<u>Living in the moment</u>

Opening the Door to a Life Less Ordinary

Life doesn't have to be a boring checklist of routine tasks. It doesn't have to be about simply "getting through the day" or "waiting for the weekend." The truth is, every day is an opportunity to live in an extraordinary way—but most of us have become experts in making the mundane safe and predictable. Let's start with a simple question: when was the last time you did something that made your heart race with excitement, or made you feel alive in a way that was so vivid, you couldn't wait to tell someone about it? It could be that you're waiting for something big to happen before you take life off autopilot. But here's the reality: waiting for the "big thing" often means you miss out on the magic that's already happening around you. The key to living interestingly isn't about waiting for big events—it's about changing the lens through which you see the world.

Rethinking Comfort Zones

Comfort zones are like warm, cozy blankets—they feel good, but they don't do much for your growth. If you want an interesting life, you have to stop clinging to what's comfortable and safe. This doesn't mean you should go jump off a cliff or completely disrupt your life (unless you're into that). But what it does mean is that you should start saying "yes" to experiences that make you feel slightly uncomfortable.

For example, consider the last time you said "yes" to something new or unfamiliar. It could have been trying a new food, taking a different route to work, or even talking to a stranger. Every time you step out of your comfort zone, your life becomes more diverse, more colorful, and definitely more interesting.

The Power of Curiosity

One of the most underrated ways to live interestingly is simply by embracing curiosity. Think about it: curiosity is the fuel for innovation, for adventure, and for personal growth. It's the reason kids are constantly asking, "Why?" It's the reason people travel the world, explore new hobbies, and push boundaries.

Instead of accepting things at face value, ask questions. Dive deeper. Explore new ideas. You'll be amazed at what you discover when you approach life with an inquisitive mind. Go on a "curiosity walk." Walk through a neighborhood or city street you've never explored, and as you do, ask yourself questions. What's the history of that old building? Who's behind that new café? What story could that street tell? Every inch of life holds fascinating answers, and the more curious you are, the more interesting the world becomes.

Pursuing Passions with Unfiltered Enthusiasm

An interesting life is one where you're passionate about something. It doesn't matter what it is— whether it's painting, rock climbing, learning a new language, or collecting vintage comic books. The more you throw yourself into your passions, the more you'll find that your life is never boring.

It's easy to get distracted by the "shoulds"—the things you feel you "have to" do because society says so. But if you start pouring energy into what really excites you, you'll find that every moment has the potential for adventure now think about a passion or hobby that you've put off. Now, make a plan to dedicate 30 minutes a day to it for a week. You'll be surprised how quickly those small moments can turn into a deeply interesting experience.

Embracing Spontaneity

Routine can be a killer when it comes to living an interesting life. Sure, routines help us stay organized, but they can also box us in. Spontaneity is where the magic happens. Think about the last spontaneous decision you made. Maybe it was a last-minute trip, calling up an old friend you hadn't spoken to in years, or simply deciding to take the long way home. Spontaneity breaks the monotony and shakes up your daily rhythms in exciting ways. I will give you an example One of the most interesting trips I ever took was to a city I'd never heard of before. I picked a random place on the map, booked a flight, and within a few hours, I was there—wandering through streets, stumbling upon hidden gems, and meeting the most fascinating people. I couldn't have planned it better if I tried.

The Art of Storytelling

Life is interesting when you have stories to tell—and the best part is that anyone can have them. It's not about waiting for life to hand you a dramatic event; it's about how you live the stories you already have. Every person you meet, every place you go, every challenge you face can turn into a story. What makes it interesting is the way you share it. Practice becoming a storyteller. Whether it's over coffee with a friend, on your blog, or at a dinner party—stories make life colorful. Start paying attention to the details in your life. Look for the humor, the drama, and the beauty in even the most ordinary experiences. The next time you tell someone about your day, see if you can turn it into a mini-adventure.

Living with Intention, Not Perfection

Let's get something straight: Living an interesting life doesn't mean living a perfect one. Perfection is overrated. Instead, live with intention. What do I mean by intention? It's about actively choosing how you show up each day. It's deciding what kind of energy you want to bring into the world and committing to it. For example, you don't have to travel the world to live an exciting life. You can make your everyday moments more interesting by living with purpose. The way you interact with people, the energy you bring to your work, your dedication to learning—these are all choices that can infuse your life with more meaning and excitement.

Nurturing Relationships That Spark Joy

Life is infinitely more interesting when you're surrounded by people who inspire, challenge, and support you. Relationships have the power to elevate your life in ways that solitary pursuits never can. Think about the people who make you feel alive. Maybe they're the ones who get you laughing until your stomach hurts, or the ones who encourage you to take risks. These are the people who bring color to your life. Invest in these relationships. Call that friend you haven't spoken to in a while. Plan a spontaneous get-together with people who lift you up. The more joy and depth you bring to your relationships, the more interesting your life becomes.

Becoming Comfortable with Change

An interesting life is one where change is embraced, not feared. The world is constantly evolving, and so are you. The best way to live interestingly is to stay flexible and open to new possibilities. Change doesn't always have to be big. It can be as simple as changing your perspective on a problem, trying a new way of working, or even introducing new hobbies into your life.

The Gift of the Present

The most incredible thing about life is that it's happening right now. Not tomorrow. Not next year. Not even the next minute. It's happening in the very moment you're reading this sentence. We've all heard the phrase "live in the moment," but how often do we actually practice it? Instead, we're constantly caught up in the past—thinking about what we could have done differently—or worrying about the future—wondering what might go wrong. But here's the secret: The only thing we ever truly have is the present. The art of living in the moment doesn't just make life easier—it makes life infinitely more interesting. The moment you stop living in a constant loop of "what was" and "what will be," you unlock the beauty of now. You become present with the world, the people around you, and yourself. That's where the magic is.

The Power of Focus

Imagine being at a concert, surrounded by hundreds of people, yet you're not really there. You're on your phone, scrolling through social media, checking messages, and planning your week. You're physically present, but mentally, you're somewhere else entirely. What if, instead of losing yourself in distractions, you fully immersed yourself in the music, the energy, the excitement of the crowd? This is what it means to live in the moment: to give your full attention to the present experience.

Focus is a superpower. It transforms an average moment into something extraordinary. Whether you're listening to a friend talk about their day, eating a meal, or taking a walk, focusing on what's in front of you makes every experience rich and meaningful. The art of being present starts with focusing on what matters now.

Let Go of Perfection

Living in the moment doesn't mean chasing perfection. In fact, the more you try to perfect every little thing, the more you miss out on the beauty of imperfection. Life isn't a script or a checklist—it's messy, chaotic, and unpredictable. And that's what makes it fascinating. When you let go of the idea that everything has to be flawless, you open yourself up to the spontaneity of life. You'll realize that some of the best moments come from the unexpected—those random conversations, the unplanned adventures, the surprise experiences that take you off course. It's the imperfection of life that gives it its texture, and when you stop fighting it, you start enjoying the ride.

Find Adventure in the Ordinary

Living in the moment isn't about waiting for life-changing events or epic vacations. The most interesting experiences are often hidden in the most ordinary moments of your daily life. Your commute to work, a conversation with a stranger, or even the feeling of sunshine on your face can become an adventure when you're fully aware and present.

Next time you're walking down the street, stop for a second and look around. Notice the colors, the sounds, the little details that make that moment unique. Instead of rushing through life, slow down. There's an entire world of wonder right at your fingertips if you stop to notice it.

Break Free from Regret and Worry

A lot of our mental energy is wasted on regret—thinking about things we've done in the past—or worry—thinking about things we have no control over in the future. But when you live in the moment, you realize how much of that energy is being used on things that don't even exist anymore, or haven't happened yet.

Regret ties you to a past that's already gone, and worry holds you hostage to a future that's out of your hands. The beauty of living in the moment is that you free yourself from both. The only time you can control is the one you're in right now. Let go of the weight of regret and the stress of what's to come, and embrace the peace that comes from being fully present.

Be Fully Present with Others

How often do you find yourself in a conversation, but your mind is somewhere else? Maybe you're thinking about your to-do list, checking your phone, or planning your next move. But when you're truly present with others, you give them the gift of your full attention, and that's one of the most meaningful things you can do.

Living in the moment is about being with people, not just in their physical presence. Listen actively, engage fully, and respond authentically. It's in these moments of connection that we experience the most profound joys of life. When you give someone your undivided attention, you also create space for deeper, more meaningful conversations and relationships.

How to Practice Mindfulness

Mindfulness is the act of paying attention to the present moment without judgment. It's the key to living fully and authentically. Practicing mindfulness doesn't mean you have to meditate for hours or become a guru. It's about bringing awareness to your everyday life.

Start small. When you're eating, focus on the taste, the texture, and the act of chewing. When you're walking, notice how your feet touch the ground, how the air feels against your skin. As you practice mindfulness, you'll find that even the simplest tasks can become profoundly interesting and enjoyable.

Embrace Spontaneity

Living in the moment also means embracing spontaneity. Instead of planning every step of your day, leave room for surprises. Say yes to the unexpected opportunities that come your way. Wander off the beaten path, both physically and metaphorically.

Spontaneity doesn't always mean doing something wild; it could be as simple as changing your routine, trying something new, or saying "yes" to an impromptu invite. When you allow life to unfold without a rigid plan, you give yourself permission to experience the unpredictable beauty that comes with living in the moment.

Let Go of Comparisons

So much of our focus is consumed by what others are doing—what they're achieving, where they're going, how they're living. But living in the moment means you're not concerned with anyone else's journey. You're not measuring your life against a standard that isn't yours.

When you stop comparing yourself to others, you allow yourself to fully experience your own life. And when you do that, you realize how rich and unique your own experiences are. No one else has your perspective, your path, or your story. Let go of comparisons and simply be.

The Joy of Presence

Living in the moment brings a deep sense of joy and fulfillment that's impossible to find in the past or future. When you are fully present in your life, you experience everything with more intensity, with more passion, and with more appreciation.

The most interesting moments of your life won't come from a carefully crafted plan or a future destination. They will come when you embrace the beauty of now—when you let go of distractions, expectations, and the need to control. The best way to live an interesting life is to embrace the moments as they come, fully and wholeheartedly.

Conclusion – The Only Thing Holding You Back is You

Ultimately, living an interesting life boils down to one simple truth: you are the creator of your own story. You can make every day as exciting, challenging, and colorful as you want it to be.

The only thing standing in the way of you living a life full of adventure and meaning is your own hesitation. The question isn't, "Can I live an interesting life?" It's, "Will I choose to make my life interesting today?"

So, let's start. The world is waiting.

X

<u>Why people changes</u>

"We can not become what we want by remaining what we are" —*Max Depree*

I have a friend like during my graduation she listens to me with a lot of patience about everything I went through but now I think that friendship is not life long as it ends with time or you should say when new people enters in our life some old faces disappear.

Female friendships are the backbone of our support systems and it is no wonder that many women share a bond as strong as sisterhood with their closest friends. They are powerful enough to change lives and enact movements. They are also quiet enough to guide and support. Female friendships are amongst the most enduring, intentional, and mutual relationships of our lives. They are safe spaces for us to be authentically ourselves, without fear of judgement and retaliation. As social theorist bell hooks put it, "We want these bonds to be honoured cherished commitments, to bind us as deeply as marriage vows."

It is a shame that society places romantic relationships and marriage at the centre of our lives, instead of friendship. By placing friendship as the number one priority of our lives, we disrupt this societal expectation of needing a man or a partner to keep us happy. In the book mentioned at the start of this article, 'Big Friendship' refers to the one major friendship that keeps you tethered to this world. Often incomprehensible to the people outside this friendship, it is the deliberate act of committed friendship. Many of us make our first friends on the playground or via the once ubiquitous 'building/society friends' of the pre-internet times. From there, I met some friends for the next ten years of our lives, we spend seven to nine hours a day with the same people, going through the same things as us. Bonds are created as a result of that, with no real effort to keep it going. For some of us though, that can be extremely traumatic, especially for those of us who are different. As someone who went to co- ed school, I have a very good time. but I was nerdy, nervous, and closeted; a perfect target for the bullies. However, my luck did a complete 180 when I was in the eighth grade. Our small group of six kept to ourselves, shared our dabbas every day, and generally wreaked havoc on our unsuspecting parents on the weekends. Suffice to say that I am only here today because of those five girls. At the age of 15, I realised what friendship with other women could do for me. Through each stage of my life since then, I have formed deeply foundational and lasting friendships with women from all walks of life. I have never felt <u>lonelier</u> than I did at the beginning of the pandemic. I was suddenly states, countries, and continents away from my otherwise ever-present girl gang. Since then, we have stayed in touch only virtually, and haven't yet managed to all meet in one place again. Nevertheless, our connection has only grown stronger with each passing day. Pre-pandemic 2020 found my group of undergrad classmates we all have a great time Mainstream media depicts female friendships as secondary to romantic relationships. Female friendships are stereotyped to sell the drama between women. But I think the difference is, that we are all simultaneously the heroes and sidekicks in our stories, and perfectly happy to play both roles.

It is a shame that society places romantic relationships and marriage at the centre of our lives, instead of friendship. By placing friendship as the number one priority of our lives, we disrupt this societal expectation of needing a man or a partner to keep us happy. In the book mentioned at the start of this article, 'Big Friendship' refers to the one major friendship that keeps you tethered to this world. Often incomprehensible to the people outside this friendship, it is the deliberate act of committed friendship. I am a hermit. I love my alone time. I prefer to be alone much of the time because my solitude is so sweet. There are certain relationships, however, where the power of connection takes over. And more recently, the power of sisterhood has played a beautiful role in my life. In the past, the idea of sisterhood sounded quite terrible to me to be honest. I've always considered myself to be different from most women. I don't like to shop or gossip. I don't watch popular TV shows or read celebrity magazines. But somehow, regardless of my unique ways, and through the many phases of life, I always managed to have few close female friends. As I evolved, a natural cleansing of old friends occurred with a welcoming of new ones. Friends tend to reflect our interests and ideas about life at any given time. The reason I've managed to connect with amazing women throughout my life is because I have been patient, discerning and always true to myself.

There's a reason I always feel so good after female bonding time–studies have shown it is good for our health. Female bonding time fights against depression and encourages healthy hormone production. And the benefits exist far beyond health. Through the changes we grow through in life, it's nice to feel loved and supported–to know that we're not in this alone.

When we share our battles and victories with others it makes this rollercoaster ride that much more enjoyable. What's even more incredible is the opportunity to play, co-create and work together. There will be times of challenges within the sisterhood too. Where we share not only what inspires us, but also what pains us. There will be tears and some disagreements as we grow to know and understand each other more deeply. But these times are worth it because our bonds become strengthened.**Having a sisterhood encourages us to stand in our power, live life, try new things and take chances.** I am not saying to go out and makes friends with every woman who crosses your path. Despite the billions of people in the world, it is quite obvious that we deeply connect with only a small percentage and rightly so because there are only so many hours in a day.

It is about quality over quantity. It's important to discern and connect with those we feel drawn to most–those who make us feel good and loved.

XI

<u>Self Love</u>

It is interesting to know the fact that human beings always try to find the better to best conditions in every moment of life so that he/she can live a happy and a good life. It is not any kind of selfishness or something like that. Basically, it is all about the limits of an individual to bear the pressure when she/he doesn't find any person who will understand them 100%. If we talk about India, there are many people who have good job, good packages, good lifestyle, good habits, good opportunity but still they are not happy (or say satisfy) 100%. So, if in life everything will be good then it doesn't give guarantee that the person will always stay happy.

Happiness is something that can be feel but not easily expressible in words or paragraph or book. Now on the other hand, there is one bitter truth also, that is, life is not so easy what we think about it. In our life too we had to go through from many risky things on daily basis, like if you are getting late to office then you will start driving fast and sometime this causes injury by a road accident, but if you will reach to your office on time after this rash driving then you would be titled as a "punctual, Disciplined and hardworking person".

And if you already have a good life either that's career or love life, why do you need to find something much better? I understand people are dreamer we dream high and never been contented but how can we finish or achieve something if we don't stick to one. Always think hundred times before doing the big decision of your life. remember regret is always at the end and looks can be deceiving. So, it is not always bad to take chance I something, only condition is that it will be good for you as well as for the other person too and no one's life will be effect by it badly. If you are happy, you have found yourself. Nobody can full-fill all wishes. If everybody full fill all his/ her wishes. Then there is no motive in life. Without the motive what's the point of life? If you are happy consider yourself luckiest person in the world. If you find happiness in whatever you do. You have found yourself. Just compare people who've found themselves with those that haven't. The common denominator is confidence, and how they carry themselves is how they wear themselves. They are comfortable in their own skin.

This has nothing to do with what type of person you are or how well you dress. You may still be arrogant, immature, incompetent, or delusional. Everyone may disagree with your taste. But at least you know who you are, you aren't afraid to show it, and you aren't insecure. Anyone who is comfortable in their skin is better off for it. At least you are confident. Just as you cannot buy confidence, you cannot buy yourself, nor can anyone give it to you. Just as no one can pick out your outfit. Except when that person knows you better than you know yourself. This is rare.

Also, think of the last time you lost confidence. It was probably when you 'lost' yourself. And when you emerged from whatever phase it was you were going through, you more than likely emerged confident. You found your new self, and this is when you know you've changed. The journey to gain confidence, whether it be your first or your last, is the same journey as finding one's self. The first time is often unintentional and temporary, and each rediscovery can be as permanent as it is intentional. As you evolve, so should you're clothing. You shouldn't always be comfortable dressing like a teen. The hardest part is overcoming what you cannot change, because we all feel stuck with what we are given. The dilemma here is that we cannot escape our own skin.

All of us have the habit of going down memory lane more often than not. Back when the internet was more of a luxury than a necessity, there were photo albums to make us feel nostalgic about how our childhood was. Thanks to the various social media platforms, these sessions are on a global level. From pop culture to cultural traditions, each of them evolves during the course of time. Time and time again, netizens come up with different and interesting ways to remember the good old days. An instance of this has been trending on all social media platforms for a day or two. It is called 'in search of gold, we lost a diamond."

In this, they put all kinds of advancement under 'gold to be searched' and the nostalgic moments under the 'diamond we lost.'It is something like 'in search of gold we lost the diamond'. This means We forget something that was precious like a diamond and find something new which is special like gold but not as diamonds. We lose something more special for just special. Intense desire or greed is a negative aspect of human character which destroys happy and prosperity in life. It is explicit that diamond is dearer than gold. The person who gives up gold in search of diamond loses everything. The import of this expression is that you should never abandon the definite thing (gold) instead of the indefinite item (diamond). This construction can be equated with the idiom ' a bird in hand is worth two in the bush'.

XII

<u>Why do we quickly lose our interest on things we were so passionate about before?</u>

We live in a world that has many, many interesting things to offer. We are bound to come across many of them throughout our journey through life. Many at first arouse our interest (or "passion"), we pursue them for a while, and then we either get bored, or find something else that interests us more, or if we had any serious aspirations, run into people that are far more talented and/or committed to that particular hobby or occupation and our interest begins to dwindle.

There is absolutely nothing wrong with any of this. I pursued many, many things with great interest and passion, but then I reached a level where I was competing against people who were far more serious and talented. I used to play chess competitively, but at some point I became good enough that I was up against people who basically spent all their spare time in pursuit of chess. As much as I loved badminton, I just did not want it to consume my life and decided to pursue other hobbies. I used to be a serious player, but the same thing happened: I could not compete against people whose life was badminton and so I gave it up.

Some points to care about :

- **Practice self-care:** If you are not taking care of yourself, meaning *both* your body and your mind, your passions and interests will suffer. Practicing self-care can help you feel better about yourself which may revive your motivation. This could be as simple as blocking out 15 minutes to read that book that's been sitting on your nightstand, or it might be taking a walk around the neighborhood every day after lunch. It might be something a little more involved like setting aside a few hours every Friday night to give yourself a little spa treatment or making sure you're getting a full night's rest. Self-care is all about making sure you have what you need physically, mentally, and emotionally to set yourself up for health and happiness.
- **Differentiate between a loss of interest and avoidance:** Lack of interest and avoidance are two very different things, and

distinguishing between the two may be helpful. When you feel yourself not wanting to do something you used to enjoy, ask yourself whether you have a loss of interest in the activity or negative feelings about the activity. Negative feelings indicate avoidance and may be a sign that you have new, negative associations with the activity. If this is the case, a professional therapist can work with you to try to identify the source of these associations.

- **Find a friend with similar hobbies:** Buddying up with somebody who shares your hobbies may bring the motivation, inspiration, and support you need when you're losing interest in everything.
- **Take a class or join a club:** Joining clubs or classes may help you reconnect with your passion, and resolve your loss of interest by giving you an opportunity to learn, enhance skills, and meet others who share your interests.
- **Take small steps toward what you once enjoyed:** If you are feeling a loss of interest, try a less extensive version of activities you usually enjoy. Even though you might not get the rush of an all-day hike, or you don't quite have that craving to pull out the mixing bowls and start measuring out ingredients, it's worth taking small steps to even minimally engage in activities you once loved. Maybe that

means going on a walk in the park instead of packing up for an all-day adventure, or popping a premixed cupcake batter in the oven instead of baking a Swedish Princess Cake from scratch — working to revive that joy by taking baby steps toward your once-favorite activities can help you slowly start enjoying those pastimes again.

- **Think about why you loved it in the first place:** Remembering the reasons you used to enjoy a certain activity or hobby may help you move past your lack of interest and get back in touch with your passions and abilities.

You may be quitting too soon!As you learn a thing, it takes a considerable time and commitment for you to master and put your skills into practical application. You are able to see your skills serving some real need. This is where real inspiration comes from. If you quit and run to the next too soon, and go on repeating the same pattern, you are then stuck in a trap. The shallow run trap ?Stay until you are a master of your current interest, and then serve with these skills which would now make an impact in the domain.Now, if you jump to the next, you could carry your skills laterally to your new interest.A master musician may acquire a new interest in painting, but never loses interest in his music. Soon, he would be a master painter too.If you move on laterally as a master, you turn versatile.Swami Vivekananda had said that if you gain knowledge over a thing, you gain power over it.How can you lose interest on something that you have considerable power over ?Be a master before you quit, if you must!!

The second name of the mind is "searching for the new".The mind is always in the curiosity of the new! You will be very surprised that for which you were very anxious, restless, after getting it, you have no interest in it. The mind always takes interest in the new and this is the identity of the mind. The day your mind is dropped then you will experience a new state, otherwise this circle will be continued.

Disclaimer : It's complicated !!

It's the nature of the human being to get something they don't have. But once you get it, sooner or later, you will lose the interest in it.

The problem is when we have something, we only see what are the negative things associated with it(may it be your job or anything), while when we don't have something, we starting looking for only positives in it. I can give you a simple example, a normal human being feels that life of celebrities is rich and luxurious. While a celebrity feels that life of a normal human being is good because people and media don't track his personal life. Both the statements are true but they're looks for only positive associated with others life. What I said till now is one part of the story. Also, the other important thing is when you say that you like something or like to have something, ask yourself that do you really need it or you want it just because of the influence of the people around you.

Inshort, grass is always greener on the other side.

Or in our language we can say that :-

Dusre ki thali me ghee jyada lagta hai .